CECILY PARSLEY'S
NURSERY RHYMES

CECILY PARSLEY'S
NURSERY RHYMES

BY

BEATRIX POTTER

Author of
"The Tale of Peter Rabbit," etc.

LONDON
FREDERICK WARNE & Co. Ltd.
AND NEW YORK

FOR LITTLE PETER
IN NEW ZEALAND

ORD EDN ISBN O 7232 0614 7
LIB EDN ISBN O 7232 0637 6

PRINTED IN GREAT BRITAIN FOR THE PUBLISHERS
BY HENRY STONE AND SON (PRINTERS) LTD., BANBURY
D6135·180

CECILY PARSLEY lived in
a pen,
And brewed good ale for
gentlemen;

GENTLEMEN came every day,
Till Cecily Parsley ran away.

GOOSEY, goosey, gander,
  Whither will you wander?
Upstairs and downstairs,
    And in my lady's cham-
    ber!

THIS pig went to market ;
This pig stayed at home ;

THIS pig had a bit of meat ;

A<small>ND</small> this pig had none ;

THIS little pig cried
    Wee ! wee ! wee !
I can't find my way home.

PUSSY-CAT sits by the
  fire ;
  How should she be fair ?
In walks the little dog,
  Says "Pussy! are you there?"

"HOW do you do, Mistress
    Pussy?
    Mistress Pussy, how do
        you do?"
"I thank you kindly, little dog,
    I fare as well as you!"

THREE blind mice, three
blind mice,
See how they run!
They all run after the farmer's
wife,
And she cut off their tails with
a carving knife,
Did ever you see such a thing
in your life
As three blind mice!

BOW, wow, wow !
  Whose dog art thou ?
"I'm little Tom Tinker's dog,
    Bow, wow, wow !"

WE have a little garden,
    A garden of our own,
And every day we water there
    The seeds that we have
    sown.

WE love our little garden,
And tend it with such care,
You will not find a faded leaf
Or blighted blossom there.

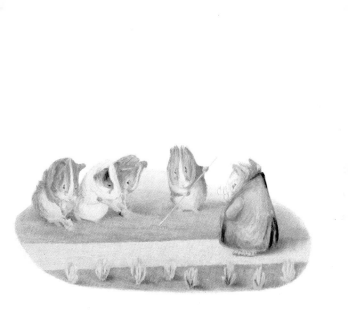

NINNY NANNY NETTI-
COAT,
In a white petticoat,
    With a red nose,—
The longer she stands,
    The shorter she grows.

Printed for the Publishers by
Henry Stone & Son (Printers) Ltd., Banbury

1768·1177